How a Dog Saved My Life

Written by Debbie Schrack
Illustrated by Kelly Smyth,
Sebastian DeLara, and Nibiya Binu

A Noah Text® Chapter Book
brought to you by Readeezy & Noah Text®

Paperback ISBN: 9781956944358

Noah Text®

The **Noah Text®** Chapter Books have been carefully selected and curated to meet the needs of all readers – and striving and struggling readers in particular – by providing superior text accessibility. Noah Text® books are rendered in **Noah Text®, a proprietary evidence-based methodology for displaying text that increases reading skill.**

Grounded in the science of reading, Noah Text® is a specialized scaffolded text that shows **syllable patterns** within words by highlighting them with bold and unbold and marking **long vowels** (vowels that "say their own names"). Here are some examples:

entertainment ⟶ **en**ter**tain**ment

beautiful ⟶ **beau**ti**ful**

photosynthesis ⟶ **pho**to**syn**the**sis**

comprehension ⟶ **com**pre**hen**sion

ironic ⟶ iron**ic**

lieutenant ⟶ **lieu**ten**ant**

achievement ⟶ **a**chieve**ment**

epitome ⟶ **e**pi**to**me

ideology ⟶ ide**ology**

coordination ⟶ **co**or**di**na**tion**

By showing readers the structure of words, Noah Text® enhances reading skills, freeing up cognitive resources that readers can devote to comprehension. Noah Text® simulates simpler writing systems (e.g., Finland's) in which learning to read is easier due to visible, predictable word patterns. As a result, Noah Text® increases reading fluency, stamina, accuracy, and confidence while building skills that transfer to plain text reading.

Highly recommended by structured literacy specialists, Noah Text® is effective for developing, struggling, and dyslexic readers and for English-language learners. Noah Text® enables resistant and struggling readers to advance their reading skills beyond basic proficiency so that they can tackle higher-level learning.

Readers find Noah Text® intuitive and easy to use, requiring little to no instruction to get started. A sound key that further explains how Noah Text® works can be found at the back of this book.

For further information on Noah Text® and its products, please visit www.noahtext.com.

Dear Parents, Educators, and Striving English-Language Readers,

As individuals develop the ability to read beyond the elementary level, their challenge is to build on a basic awareness of how patterns of letters stand for sounds and how those sounds come together to make words. Readers who learn the letter patterns in one-syllable words are poised to recognize them in longer, multisyllable words.

For struggling readers, however, long words can appear to be a sea of individual letters whose syllable sub-divisions are hard to discern. The Noah Text® series highlights where syllable breaks occur, while also signaling long vowels -- those that "say their own names." These visual cues help struggling readers decode words more easily and read more fluently and accurately.

Now, with Noah Text® Chapter Books, all individuals can learn to read with less effort, empowering them to experience enriching literature and enlightening informational texts.

Miriam Cherkes-Julkowski, Ph.D.
Professor, Educational Psychology (retired)
Educational Diagnostician and Consultant

How a Dog Saved My Life

Written by Debbie Schrack
Illustrated by Kelly Smyth,
Sebastian DeLara, and Nibiya Binu

A Noah Text® Chapter Book
brought to you by Readeezy & Noah Text®

CONTENTS

FIGHT!

CHAPTER ONE

It was only fireworks. Can you believe it?

Six kids, including me, ended up in the hospital because some dummy decided to shoot off firecrackers in the middle of a hallway fight.

Here's how it all went down. It was Friday, lunch time. My best friend Mo and I were at our lockers, planning a trip over the weekend to a new skate park that just opened near my house. And then there was shouting up the hall, and someone yelled "Fight!" Kids started streaming by us to catch the action, chattering in excitement.

“It’s **prob**a**bly** **Dev**in Rose **a**gain,” Mo said, **clos**ing his **lock**er. “You **wan**na go watch, **Bob**by?”

Devin Rose was the **big**gest **bul**ly at **West**lake High. Not a day went by that he **did**n’t try to pick a fight with **some**one. **Thank**ful**ly**, he had **nev**er **sin**gled out Mo or me. We made a point to stay **un**der his **ra**dar.

“Nah,” I said. “I’m **hun**gry. Let’s go to lunch.”

We turned and **head**ed in the **oth**er **di**rec**tion**. Mr. Pitt, our **prin**ci**pal**, passed us with a **wor**ried look, **fol**lowed by Coach **Wil**son. **Dev**in Rose is the **quar**ter**back** on our **foot**ball team and Coach **Wil**son is the **on**ly **re**ason **Dev**in **has**n't been kicked out of school yet.

We **al**most made it to the **cafe**fe**te**ri**a**.

There was a loud bang up the hall where the fight was, and then two more. BANG! BANG! **Some**one yelled "Gun!"

I **al**most had a heart **at**tack. **Eve**ry**one start**ed **run**ning and **scream**ing. Mo's a **sprint**er on the track team and he took off **a**head of me. I tried to keep up, but I'm not an **athl**ete. Golf is more my speed. My heart was **pound**ing out of my chest and my legs felt like lead. With each step that passed I got **slow**er and **slow**er, like I was **run**ning through **quick**sand. It **did**n't take long for a mob of **sweat**y kids to **sur**round me, all **fran**tic to get to the front doors of the school. I could **bare**ly breathe in the crush of **bod**ies **push**ing and **pull**ing me **eve**ry which way.

"Mo!" I yelled. "Mo!"

But I **could**n't see him **an**y**more**. I tripped **o**ver **some**one's foot and went down. That's the last thing I **re**mem**ber un**til I woke up in the **am**bu**lance**.

When I fell, it was like **dominos**. Kids piled on top of kids, and I was all the way at the **bot**tom. The **E**R doc said I was **re**a**lly luck**y that I just **end**ed up with a **con**cus**sion**. It could have been a lot worse. Still, **eve**ry time I think **a**bout what **hap**pened I get this **pan**ick**y feel**ing **in**side like there's a swarm of bees **buzz**ing **a**round my **stom**ach.

the whole weekend? u serious???

I stayed in the **hos**pi**tal Fri**day night for **ob**ser**va**tion. My **ep**ic **weekend** with Mo turned out to be a non-**start**er. Mom and Dad **would**n't **e**ven let Mo come **o**ver, which was **prob**a**bly** for the best since I had a **mon**ster **head**ache.

Now it's **Mon**day and my **head**ache is gone, but I still have that **pan**ick**y feel**ing. How am I **supp**osed to go to school and act like **noth**ing's **hap**pened?

EXIT

Mom drops me off which is great **be**cause I was too **jit**ter**y** to walk to school. Mo meets me at the front door. We head to the **cafeteria** to grab a **dough**nut **be**fore first **pe**ri**od** just like we **al**ways do. I've **eat**en a **Bos**ton Cream **eve**ry day since the first day of school, but **to**day I can't **stom**ach it. The **cafeteria** is too **crowd**ed. Too **cra**zy. **Anytime some**one yells or bangs their tray on a **ta**ble, I jump in my seat like I just got **Ta**sered.

RINGGGG!
GO! Champions!
Treat Others The Way You Want To Be Treated!
ELECTVIE FAIR

The bell rings and my **anxie**ty **lev**el flies off the charts.

“You **o**kay, **Bob**by?” Mo says. “You look kind of pale.

I’m not **o**kay. Not **e**ven close. But I’m too **em**bar**rassed** to tell Mo how scared I am. I don’t want him to think I’m a **gi**ant **ba**by. **Eve**ry**one** else in school is **act**ing like **noth**ing’s happened. What’s wrong with me?

“Nah, I’m good.” With **trem**bling **fin**gers, I grab my **back**pack off the floor. “Let’s go.”

EVERYONE TO
THE AUDITORIUM!

When we walk out of the **caf**e**te**ri**a** and **in**to the hall, I break **in**to a sweat. It's **e**ven **loud**er out here and I swear the hall is **nar**row**er** than it used to be. What will **hap**pen if **some**one sets off **an**oth**er** **fire**crack**er**? I mean, they **nev**er caught the **per**son who did it. **May**be he or she is **plan**ning to do it **a**gain. Will **eve**ry**one** start **run**ning and...

A voice blasts out of the **o**ver**head** **spea**ker, and I jump a mile.

"Did you hear that?" Mo says. "Pitt wants us all to go to the **au**di**to**rium. He **prob**a**bly** wants to talk **a**bout what **hap**pened on **Fri**day."

MATH
FIRST BASKET-
BALL GAME!
Dance
Come Join

I can't wrap my head **a**round it. The whole school in one room, packed in like **sar**dines? Is he **se**ri**ous**?

I push past Mo. "Save me a seat. I'm **go**ing to the **bath**room."

Mo's jaw drops. "For **re**al, dude?"

"I—I'll be there in a **mi**nute."

I head for the **bath**room, but **be**fore I get there I turn and look back. There is no sign of Mo. I walk right past the **bath**room and out the front doors of the school.

CHAPTER TWO

Guess where I am? **Af**ter**noon** **de**ten**tion**.

That's not **e**ven the worst part. **Dev**in Rose is **sit**ting right **be**hind me. He keeps **throw**ing **spit**balls at me and **call**ing me "**Bob**by the **Ba**by" **un**der his breath. This is a **ter**ri**ble** turn of **e**vents. How did I **e**ven end up on **Dev**in **Rose**'s **ra**dar? I swear he can smell fear. That's how he picks his **vic**tims. And **ev**er since the day I got crushed in the crowd **af**ter his fight, I've been **ter**ri**fied**.

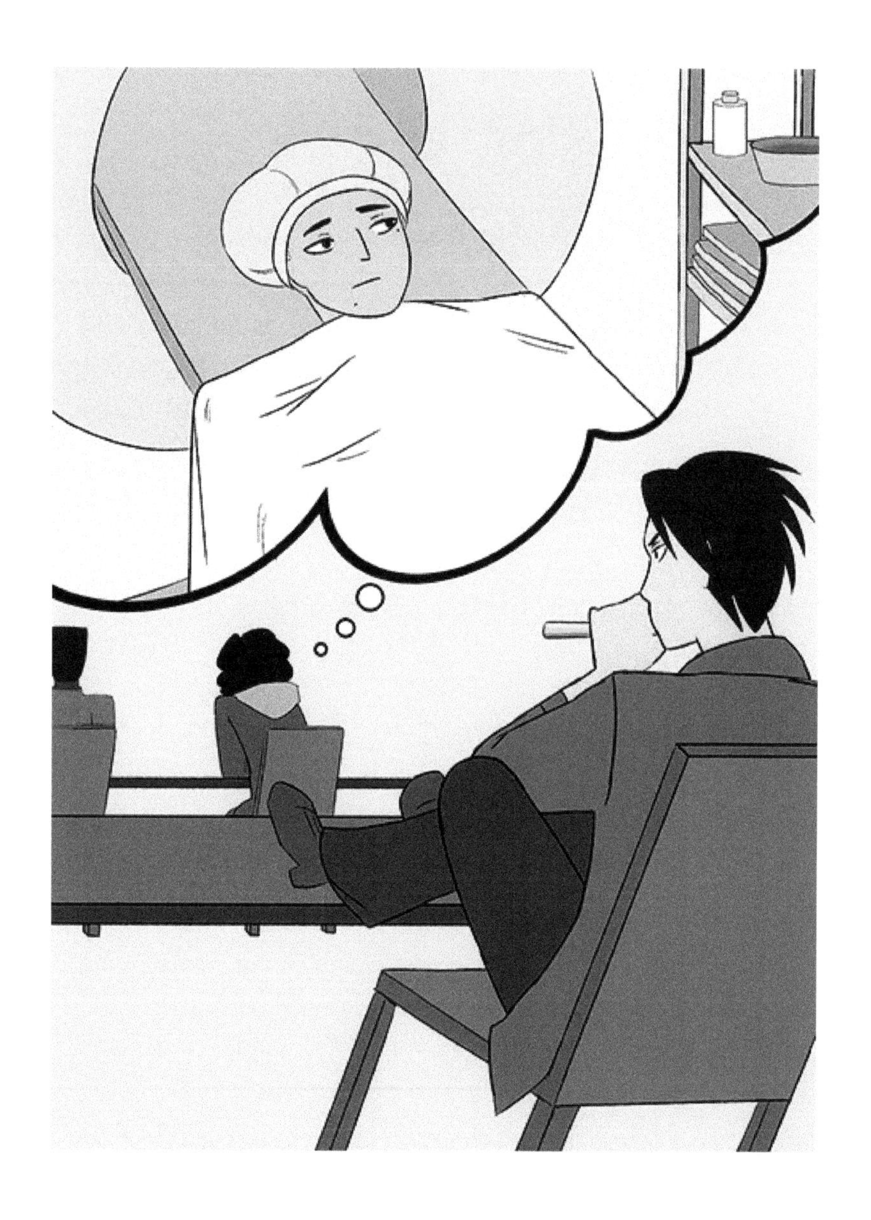

It's been **o**ver a week since it **hap**pened. That first day, when I bailed on school, I **con**vinced my mom that my **head**ache had come back. She let me stay home for a **cou**ple of days. **E**ven took me for an **M**R**I**. But when that came back **neg**a**tive** (which meant there was **noth**ing wrong with me), she **start**ed **giv**ing me weird looks. So I went back to school. What else could I do?

Anoth**er spit**ball hits the back of my head. **Bob**by **snick**ers. My **stom**ach **clutch**es. The **li**brar**y** is **hot**ter than a **sau**na. And it's so **crowd**ed. Sweat **trick**les down the back of my neck. We still have **thir**ty **mi**nutes to go. It might as well be **for**ev**er**.

When I got back to school, Mo told me that Mr. Pitt said he was **beef**ing up **se**cu**ri**ty in the halls to **a**void **an**oth**er** "**in**ci**dent**." **In**ci**dent**, ha. More like a **hor**ror show. **Anyway**, I **fig**ured he was just **blow**ing smoke. Boy, was I wrong. **Dur**ing third **pe**ri**od to**day, one of his new **se**cu**ri**ty guards caught me **hid**ing in the **bath**room **in**stead of **tak**ing an **al**ge**bra** test. This dude was **scar**y. Buzz cut, **tat**tooed arms. He looked like The Rock. And he must have been deaf, too. **Be**cause he **did**n't **lis**ten to **an**y of my **ex**cu**ses**. Just took me straight to Mr. Pitt, who gave me **af**ter**noon** **de**ten**tion**.

SCAREDY CAT!!

Twenty-five **mi**nutes to go.

Something hits me in the back, **big**ger than a **spit**ball this time. I glance at the floor. A **crum**pled piece of **note**book **pa**per lies next to my foot. I pick it up and smooth it out. On the **pa**per, **Dev**in has **writ**ten "**Scared**y cat!" and drawn a **pic**ture of a **fire**crack**er** with the word "Boom!" **un**der**neath** it.

My face gets hot, and my hands go cold. How does **Dev**in know there's **some**thing wrong with me? My **par**ents don't **e**ven know yet. I think Mo **sus**pects but he's too nice to say **any**thing. But is it that **obvi**ous? Does the whole school know what a wreck I am? It's like I have a **gi**ant "L" for **los**er stamped on my **fore**head.

AAAAHHHHHHH!!

I jump out of my seat.

Ms. **My**ers, the **li**brar**i**an, flicks a glance at me. “Sit down, **Bob**by.”

But I can’t. The walls are **clos**ing in on me. I have to get out of here.

Ms. **My**ers stands up. “I said, sit down.” Her voice is sharp.

Devin Rose starts to laugh. And **sud**den**ly** it’s like the whole world is **laugh**ing at me. The sound **ris**es and swells and fills my brain **un**til I can’t stand it **anymore**. I put my hands **o**ver my ears and start to scream.

I don't **re**mem**ber** how I end up in the **nurse**'s **of**fice. **Eve**ry**thing** is **qui**et. I'm on a cot, **un**der**neath** a **blan**ket. My hands are still **o**ver my ears. Did I just have a **ma**jor freak out in the **li**brar**y**? The last thing I **re**mem**ber** is **Dev**in Rose **laugh**ing...

I take my hands off my ears. **Some**one is **talk**ing in the **oth**er room. I think it's Mr. Cruz, my **guid**ance **coun**se**lor**. And—oh, no. Not my **par**ents. They are **go**ing to kill me.

The next thing I know, they're all in the room, **star**ing down at me. My **par**ents don't look mad, though. They seem more like **wor**ried.

"**Bob**by," Mom says. Her hair is **mess**y, and her eyes are red.

I sit up on the cot so that my legs **dan**gle **o**ver the edge, and **won**der for a **sec**ond what **hap**pened to my shoes.

"Mom, Dad, I'm **sor**ry," I say.

Mr. Cruz sits down next to me on the cot. He's an **old**er guy, **go**ing gray. He **push**es his **sil**ver-rimmed **glass**es up his nose.

"There's no need to be **sor**ry, son," he says. "I'm **fair**ly **cer**tain that you had a **pan**ic **at**tack. Your **par**ents tell me you were in the thick of things **dur**ing that **in**ci**dent** in the **hall**way a few days **a**go. Got a **con**cus**sion**."

It all comes back to me **a**gain—the loud bangs, the kids **scream**ing, the crush of **peo**ple on top of me...

My hands start to shake. "I know it **was**n't a **re**al gun, Mr. Cruz. But for a few **mi**nutes it was **re**al. I—I thought I was **go**ing to get shot—"

"Why **did**n't you tell us you were **feel**ing this way?" Mom asks.

"I thought **some**thing was wrong with me, Mom. I thought I was a freak."

"You're not a freak," Mr. Cruz says. "You have what's called **P**T**S**D—Post **Trau**mat**ic** Stress **Dis**or**der**. It **hap**pens when a **per**son like **your**self **ex**pe**ri**enc**es** a **fright**en**ing** **e**vent."

"What can we do?" Dad asks.

"**Coun**sel**ing** will help," Mr. Cruz **re**plies. "But—I have **an**oth**er** id**ea**."

"What is it?" I say. "I'll try **any****thing**."

He smiles. "I think you'd be a great **can**di**date** for a **ther**a**py** dog."

CHAPTER THREE

My **ther**a**py** dog is a black lab named **Oll**ie. He stands **a**bout two feet tall at his **shoul**der and weighs **six**ty pounds. His fur is the **col**or of **char**coal, and his eyes are **car**a**mel** brown. Oh, and have I **men**tioned that he's **su**per cool?

It took a **cou**ple of weeks to get **Oll**ie, but Mr. Cruz says I was **re**al**ly** **luck**y to get him so fast. It just so **hap**pened that the **lo**cal **Ca**nine **Com**pan**ions**, who train **ther**a**py** dogs, had **Oll**ie **a**vail**a**ble **af**ter **an**oth**er** **own**er changed his mind at the last **mi**nute. When **Oll**ie and I met, we just clicked. This might be the best thing that's **ev**er **hap**pened to me.

I **have**n't been back to school since my **pan**ic **at**tack, but I've been **bus**y. I've been **go**ing to a **doc**tor who Mr. Cruz said would help me with my **PTS**D. He wrote me a **pre**scrip**tion** for a **ther**a**py** dog. **Is**n't that **fun**ny? It's like **Oll**ie is my **med**i**cine**.

I've **al**so been **go**ing **eve**ry day to **Ca**nine **Com**pan**ions** to work with **Oll**ie and his **train**er. There's so much to learn **a**bout **tak**ing care of a dog. But there's **al**so a ton of stuff to learn **a**bout how he's **go**ing to take care of me.

Mo has been **stop**ping by my house **eve**ry day to bring me my **home**work. **To**day when he comes, I **in**tro**duce** him to **Ol**lie, who is stretched out at my feet. Mo **reach**es a hand down to pet him, but I stop him.

"We're not **sup**posed to treat him like a **regular** dog," I say. "He's a **work**ing dog. **Tak**ing care of me is his job now."

Mo laughs. "You should find the kid that set off those **fire**crack**ers** and give him a high five, dude. You've **al**ways **want**ed a dog."

"Right?" I look down at **Ol**lie. I still can't **be**lieve how this **hap**pened so fast.

Mo sits down in a chair **a**cross from me. "You **re**a**lly** think he's **go**ing to help?"

"Are you **kid**ding? **Ol**lie's **a**ma**zing**. His **trai**n**er** took us to the mall **yes**ter**day** and as soon as **Ol**lie sensed I was **get**ting **anx**ious in the crowd he **start**ed **whin**ing and **nudg**ing me to go down a hall where there were **few**er **peo**ple. I stood there and did some deep **breath**ing, and in a few **mi**nutes, I was fine."

"Wow, that's **cra**zy! So, are you **read**y to go back to school **to**mor**row**?"

I **hesitate**. "I know that **Ol**lie will help me with my **PTS**D. But what **a**bout **Dev**in Rose?"

Mo waves his hand. "Don't **wor**ry **a**bout him. It's been two weeks. I'm sure he's moved on to his next **vic**tim by now."

The first **cou**ple of days back, I’m sure that Mo is right. **Strange**ly, **Dev**in Rose is not **a**round to **both**er me. And, **al**though it’s a **lit**tle **awk**ward **tak**ing a dog to my **class**es, **eve**ry**one** is **ac**cept**ing** of **Ol**lie. I mean, it’s no **dif**fer**ent** than if I were blind and had a **see**ing-eye dog, right? There are **ther**a**py** dogs for all kinds of **prob**lems.

On the third day, though, **dis**as**ter** strikes. **Be**cause **sud**den**ly Dev**in Rose is **eve**ry**where**. Turns out he was on a **col**lege **vis**it in **an**oth**er** state. And he **has**n't **for**got**ten a**bout me or moved on to a new **vic**tim.

I think he **act**u**al**ly **mem**or**ized** my **sched**ule. **Be**cause he finds me **af**ter **eve**ry class and **foll**ows me down the hall **call**ing me "**Ba**by" and "**Sis**sy" and **oth**er words that are **e**ven worse. I'm **shak**ing by the time we get to lunch. **Oll**ie keeps **whin**ing and **nudg**ing me with his nose. He knows I'm close to a **pan**ic **at**tack.

Which is why I should **nev**er have gone **in**to the **caf**e**te**ri**a**. I thought I would be safe there, that **Dev**in **would**n't try **some**thing in such a **crowd**ed place. I **for**got he likes an **au**di**ence**.

"**Fraid**y cat," he **snick**ers **be**hind me as I get in line for school lunch. When I **ig**nore him, he **push**es me hard in the back. I **al**most knock down the girl **stand**ing in front of me.

"Stop it," I say, **turn**ing to **Dev**in.

His grin is pure **e**vil. The dude **e**ven looks like the **dev**il—he has dark hair and eyes, and **al**ways wears black, **ex**cept on game days. "What's wrong, **Bob**by? Are you scared?"

"I'm not—"

He puts his hands **o**ver his ears, just like I did when I was **hav**ing my **pan**ic **at**tack. "Help me, help me," he squeals. "I'm scared of school **be**cause **some**one set off a **fire**crack**er**."

The kids **a**round us laugh. **Eve**ry**one** in the **cafe**te**ria** has stopped to watch. My hands clench and my face flames. **Ol**lie starts to whine.

I step out of line and **Dev**in blocks our way. **Ol**lie moves in front of me and lets out a low growl. **Dev**in takes a step back. "What, so you need a dog to **pro**tect you? Jeez, what a **los**er."

"Leave us **al**one," I **stam**mer.

Devin laughs. He **pac**es in front of me, **keep**ing an eye on **Ol**lie.

A crowd **gath**ers **a**round us. I look for Mo or **an**oth**er** **friend**ly face, but I can't see **anyone** I know. **Some**one yells "Fight!" and that whole **hor**ri**ble** day comes back to me in a rush. The room starts to spin...

Ollie barks and **nudg**es my hand.

"I have to go," I say. My **breath**ing is **get**ting **rasp**y, and I think I might throw up. Why is it so hot in here?

"Let him go, **Dev**in," **some**one in the crowd says. "He looks sick."

The **se**cu**ri**ty guard who put me in **de**ten**tion** **push**es through the crowd. "What's **go**ing on here? **Eve**ry**one**, get back to your **ta**bles."

Devin smirks and waves his hand at me. "Fine. **What**ev**er**. Leave, you big **ba**by."

Boy, am I glad that **se**cu**ri**ty guard showed up. But why is he **walk**ing **a**way **al**read**y**? Does he **really** think **Dev**in will **lis**ten to him? I have to get out of here. Like **yes**ter**day**.

We **al**most make it. I'm just **slink**ing by **Dev**in when he grabs a **car**ton of milk off **some**one's tray and dumps it all **o**ver my head. I gasp as the **cold**ness seeps down the back of my neck. I can't breathe...

Every**thing af**ter that **hap**pens in slow **mo**tion. The **cafeteria e**rupts with **laugh**ter and **Oll**ie's **pull**ing me to the door and I **stum**ble **in**to the **hall**way. **Some**one grabs my arm but I'm **fall**ing and then the world goes black.

CHAPTER FOUR

I wake to **Oll**ie **lick**ing my face. Mo is **lean**ing **o**ver me.

"**Bob**by, are you **o**kay?" he asks.

"I—what **hap**pened?"

"I got to the **cafeteria** just in time to see **Dev**in Rose pour milk all **o**ver you. You were kind of **los**ing it and **Oll**ie pulled you out of the **cafeteria**. I **foll**owed you guys and then you **faint**ed…"

It all comes back then—**Dev**in **push**ing me **in**to that girl and **dump**ing milk on my head, **Oll**ie **growl**ing, and **ever**y**one** in the **cafete**ria **laugh**ing their heads off. At me.

I have **nev**er been one of the cool kids. I go to class, hang **a**round with Mo, and try not to **em**bar**rass** **my**self on the golf team. I get **ver**y **lit**tle **at**ten**tion,** and I like it that way. But now the whole school knows who I am, and I'm **noth**ing but a big joke.

"I hate **Dev**in Rose," I say.

"If it makes you feel **an**y **bet**ter, the **se**cu**ri**ty guard took him to the **of**fice."

"You know he won't get in **trou**ble. There's a big game on **Fri**day." I **scram**ble to my feet. "I'm **go**ing home."

"You don't have to," Mo says. "I have an old shirt in my **lock**er you can wear."

"It's not that. I just—can't be here **an**y**more**."

"You should at least get lunch first. You're **re**al**ly** pale."

"I'm not **go**ing back in there," I say, **look**ing at the **caf**e**te**r**ia** doors. "I was just **hu**mil**i**a**ted** in front of the whole school."

"Let's go hang in the **li**br**a**r**y** then. We can get a pass from Mr. Cruz. We'll sit there **un**til we **fig**ure this whole thing out."

"What whole thing?"

"How to take down **Dev**in Rose."

The next day when I get up for school, I'm a **jit**ter**y** mess. Can I **re**al**ly** walk **in**to that **cafete**ria **a**gain, **e**ven with Mo **be**hind me? I can't take much more **hu**mili**ation**. **Would**n't it be **bet**ter if my mom **home**schooled me? Or I **trans**ferred to a **pri**vate school?

Just then, **Oll**ie **nudg**es my hand, and I reach down and put my hand on his head. As soon as I touch his soft fur, my **jit**ters **sub**side. **Oll**ie **was**n't scared of **Dev**in **yes**ter**day**. Not one **lit**tle bit. He stepped in front of me and growled at him. If **Oll**ie can face **Dev**in Rose, then so can I.

When I get to school, Mo meets us at the front door.

"**Dev**in's in the **caf**e**te**ri**a**," he says.

"**Al**read**y**? I–thought I would wait **un**til lunch."

"No time like the **pres**ent, dude."

Again, I **se**cond guess **my**self and **a**gain I reach down and touch **Ol**lie's fur. It's **go**ing to be **o**kay. With **Ol**lie and Mo by my side, I can do this.

"**O**kay," I say. "Let's do it."

My heart in my throat, we walk **in**to the **caf**e**te**ri**a**.

Inside, it's mid-**lev**el **cha**os. **Dev**in's **a**cross the room, **sit**ting at a **ta**ble full of **foot**ball **play**ers with his back to me. I break out in a cold sweat. As I inch **slow**ly **a**round the **pe**rim**e**ter of the room, I'm glad that no one pays **an**y **at**ten**tion** to me.

Just as I'm **a**bout to reach **Dev**in's **ta**ble, Mo **ap**pears **hold**ing a **car**ton of milk. He hands it to me.

Go for it," he **whis**pers.

I stare down at the **car**ton of milk in my hand. It seemed like a good **id**e**a** when we talked it **o**ver in the **li**brar**y** **yes**ter**day**. **Pay**back. An eye for an eye. But now it just seems mean. It's not me. I don't want to be like **Dev**in Rose.

One of the **foot**ball **play**ers at **Dev**in's **ta**ble sees me and says **some**thing to **Dev**in. **Dev**in turns.

"What the...?" **Dev**in jumps out of his chair. He sees the **car**toon of milk in my hand and laughs. "Were you **go**ing to throw that milk on me? I **did**n't know you had it in you."

I can **bare**ly hear him **o**ver the **pound**ing of my heart, but when I **re**ply my voice is calm. "No, **be**cause I'm not a jerk like you are."

He walks **to**ward me with his fists up. "I'm **go**ing to pound you **in**to the ground for that."

Ollie steps in front of me and growls at **Dev**in.

Devin throws up his hands in **frus**tra**tion**. "Are you **al**ways **go**ing to hide **be**hind that dog?"

"Why? Are you scared?" I say.

Someone laughs, and **Dev**in's face **flush**es. A crowd has **gath**ered **a**round us, and kids are **mur**mur**ing**. **Pan**ic **ris**es in me, but I push it **a**way.

"I don't need to hide **be**hind **an**y**one**." I turn and hand **Ol**lie's leash and the **car**ton of milk to Mo.

Devin puts up his fists. "Let's go, then."

"Sure, I'll fight you," I say. "And you'll win **be**cause you're **big**ger than me. That's what you do, **Dev**in. You **on**ly pick on kids that are **small**er than you. **Be**cause you're a **bul**ly and **bul**lies are **cow**ards."

Devin's eyes are wide, and his face is a deep **pur**ple. "You think I'm scared of you?"

"**Eve**ry**one's** scared of **some**thing. I know I am. I thought I was **go**ing to die that day when the **fire**crack**ers** went off. I have Post **Trau**mat**ic** Stress **Dis**or**der** now. That's why I need a **ther**a**py** dog. You think it's cool to pick on kids with **dis**a**bili**ti**es**?"

Devin looks **a**round at the crowd as if he's **look**ing for **some**one to **res**cue him. No one says a word.

"**Sis**sy," he says.

He takes a step **to**ward me. I am **a**bout to die.

BEEP! BEEP! BEEP! A **hor**ri**ble** sound **ac**com**pa**nied by **flash**ing lights floods my brain and I clap my hands **o**ver my ears. It's the fire **a**larm. **Dev**in points his **fin**ger at me and laughs, just as the **sprin**klers in the **ceil**ing **activate** and **wa**ter sprays **eve**ry**where**. **Eve**ry**one** starts **scream**ing and **stam**ped**ing** out of the **cafe**te**ria**. It's my worst **night**mare all **o**ver **a**gain.

I try to move but my feet must be glued to the floor. Then Mo grabs my arm. "Let's get out of here!" His hair is **plas**tered to his **fore**head.

I **fran**ti**cal**ly look **a**round. "But where's **Ol**lie?"

"I don't know. I dropped the leash when the **sprin**klers went off."

My heart **lurch**es. "Mo! How could you?"

"Don't **wor**ry. We'll find him on the way out."

We **stum**ble **to**ward the **ex**it, **try**ing not to slip in the **pud**dles on the floor. Kids are **push**ing and **shov**ing and **pro**gress is slow. I still can't see **Ol**lie **an**y**where**. My breaths come hard and fast, but I'm **de**ter**mined** not to have a **pan**ic **at**tack.

At the door, Mo turns to check on me and his eyes **wid**en.

"**Bob**by, look!" he says, **point**ing.

As the last of the kids **scram**ble out of the **caf**e**te**ria, there's **on**ly one kid left **be**sides us. It's **Dev**in. He's on the floor in the **mid**dle of the room, passed out cold. He must have slipped in the **wa**ter and **fall**en. **Ol**lie's **be**side him, **whim**per**ing** and **push**ing him and **lick**ing his face. All of a **sud**den, the **sprin**klers stop and the **a**larm goes off. **Si**rens wail **out**side.

Devin stirs and **Ol**lie lets out a short, sharp bark. By the time we reach them, **Dev**in's **sit**ting up, his arm **a**round **Ol**lie. Mo and I grab **Dev**in's arms and help him stand. He has a bump on his **fore**head and his eyes are **glass**y.

We walk out **to**geth**er**, **Dev**in's arms **a**round our **shoul**ders. The rest of the school is out on the front lawn **watch**ing as **fire**fight**ers** with long **hos**es spray the roof. **Ho**ly cow! There **re**al**ly** was a fire.

Coach **Wil**son spies us and **hur**ries **o**ver. “Thank **heav**ens,” he says, **tak**ing **Dev**in’s arm. “I got him from here, **fel**las.”

Just as they turn **a**way, **Dev**in looks back at me.

“Thanks, **Bob**by,” he says. “I think your dog might have saved my life.”

“No **wor**ries,” I say, **grin**ning. I reach down and touch **Ol**lie’s soft fur. “I think he saved mine, too.”

Sound Key

How Noah Text® Works

Noah Text® allows readers to see sound-parts within words, providing a way for struggling readers to decode and enunciate words that are difficult to access. In turn, their improvement in reading accuracy and fluency frees up cognitive resources that they can devote to comprehending the meaning of the text, enabling them to truly enjoy reading while building their reading skills.

Syllables

A *syllable* is a unit of pronunciation with only one vowel sound, with or without surrounding consonants. Syllables line up with the way we speak and are an integrated unit of speech and hearing. Teachers often clap out syllables with their students.

Noah Text® acts upon words with more than one syllable. In a multiple-syllable word, the presentation of each syllable alternates bold, not bold, bold, etc. For example, the word "syllable" would be presented as "**syl**la**ble**," while the word "sound" is not changed at all.

Vowels

A *long vowel* is a vowel that pronounces its own letter name. Here are some examples of underlined long vowels you will find in Noah Text®, along with syllable breaks that are made obvious:

Long (a)

plate, pain, **hes**it**ate**, **na**tion

hair, rare, **par**ent, **li**brar**y**

pale, fail, **de**tail

tray, **al**ways

Long (e)

feet, teach, **com**plete

feel, deal, **ap**peal

ear, fear, here, **dis**ap**pear**, **se**vere

Long (i)

tribe, like, night, **high**light

fire, **ad**mire, **re**quire

mile, pile, **a**while, **rep**tile

Long (o)

globe, nose, **sup**pose, **re**mote

coach, whole, coal, goal, **ap**proach

mow, blown, **win**dow

Long (u)

huge, mule, **fu**el, **per**fume, **a**muse

hue, **ar**gue, **tis**sue, blue, **pollution**

Disclaimer: As noted in the research provided at noahtext.com, the English writing system is extremely complex. Thus, the process of segmenting syllables, identifying rime patterns, and highlighting long vowels, is not only tedious but ambiguous at times based on the pronunciation of various regional dialects, the complexity of English orthography, and other articulatory considerations. Noah Text® strives to be as accurate as possible in developing clear, concise modified text that will assist readers; however, it cannot guarantee universal agreement on how all words are pronounced.

Milton Keynes UK
Ingram Content Group UK Ltd.
UKHW050219021124
450537UK00013B/79